These Things I Know To Be True

Eve Sidikman

To Jonas, my muse,
Lucy, my best friend in the world,
and to Iris.
Stay weird.

The leaves turned auburn as I sat, staring out into the beautiful sunset before me. It seemed a million miles away, yet so close I could graze it with my fingers. The hill was cool and hard under me, drawing me to the musky earth. I stared out at our small village, all that was left of District 19 these days. The houses small, the food stale and scarce. What a shame. But I suppose it was all for a reason. Why give us the riches that the other districts had? Still, the wind danced through my light tunic, and my bare feet wriggled on the exposed ground.

"Hey, Ears!" called a voice from the distance. I turned around to see, of course, May. He swung his long legs in my direction, eating the ground with his huge gait. I instinctively ran my hands through my long dark hair, trying to cover my ears as best I can. Of course the action is in vain.

"How did you find me?" I asked, not really curious.

He had laughter in his voice as he replied, "Really? Really? Because I had to search our entire sprawling district to find you."

"I swear, if you start on that again…"

"I won't, don't worry. I'm just saying, this seems unfair. To just be born into being poor when I could have been born into a life where I hardly had to try to survive."

"But don't you think they have a reason?"

"I think when the districts were first formed, they had a reason. Now we're just caged animals."

"Okay, okay. Point taken. I just wish I had a winter coat."

"Here, have mine," he said, and wrapped his coat around my shoulders. I stared up into his eyes, the most unique I had ever seen. One green as the grass fields in summer, the other deep and blue as the ocean. He smiled faintly at me, and his light brown hair fell in his eyes. He blew it off by pointing his mouth at it and blowing as hard as he could. I laughed and fell onto his shoulder. He stayed still, and we sat there, staring out at the fading sunset.

As I stepped into our hut, I smelled the enticing smell of deer and roots coming at me. As I took the three strides that I had to to get across the cabin to the kitchen, I saw my dad come in through the back. I then heard rustling and another woman can in with him.

"Hey Dad, Hey Sar," I said, leaning in to smell the stew.

Dad turned towards me and waved, a familiar greeting from him. It wasn't that he was being cold, it was just that ever since Mom died, he hasn't talked much. He took the wooden spoon next to the stove and stirred the soup.

"Smells good," I said, and he nodded.

"Did you guys shoot the deer?" I asked, this time turning to Sar, our close family friend and my honorary mother.

"Yeah," she replied, "It took us most of the morning, but I have a feeling that it will be worth it."

Dad motioned with his head, and Sar and I sat at the table as he put our dinner on the table. We ate mostly in silence, letting the heat of the stew and the plumpness of the meat warm our aching stomachs. It's the first time that we've had meat in weeks. Or rather, our own meat. May is always out hunting for his family and ours.

At the end of the meal, Dad clears his throat and opens his mouth. Sar and I turn to him in surprise.

"I have to go to a meeting tomorrow, I will be back when I can"

Sar and I nod, not wanting to interrupt him. To me, his words are gold that my ears crave.

That night, I sat alone on the top of our hut. I can hear Sar and Dad whispering silently below me, but I don't have the energy to listen. I stare at the stars, the official constellations and my own made up ones. They say before The Change that there was so much pollution that they couldn't even see the stars clearly. That seems like a shame to me. The stars are my comfort, and I don't think I'll ever tire of staring at them. I close my eyes, and slowly drift off to sleep.

The next morning, I'm setting out to go look for berries when my head starts to hurt. I ignore it, and am just at the edge of the woods when it gets worse. Colors explode before my eyes, and I have to lean against a tree to stay upright. Then, everything clears and the world is in high definition. But the view isn't mine. I see a small boy, no older than ten, lying on the ground with his silver hair forming a halo about his head. Then, a man enters the room and the boy cries out in fright. He pulls his knees up to his chin, wrapping himself as tightly as possible. The man reaches into a dark corner and pulls out a whip. I can see the boy's entire body shaking. He then cracks the whip down on the boy, leaving dark red welts on his pale skin. I hear the boy cry out, his voice slashing through my ears like a knife. Tears stream down his face, but the man pulls back the whip and brings it down on the boy again and again. The muscles in his face are tight, and I can see the anger in his eyes. I reach down to pull him off the boy, but as soon as I touch him the world goes black.

Then I'm back in the forest, my eyes feeling as if someone poked them out then put them back in again. I sunk to the ground, staring at the tree in front of me. What had just happened? Those memories weren't mine. I couldn't even see the boy's face, but I could tell they were in one of the richer districts, maybe Three or Four. Who was he? Who was the man beating him? Why? I completed the rest of my task in complete and utter silence, staring blankly at things, as if they might give me answers.

When I arrived back at the village, I headed straight for May's house. I knocked lightly on the door, hoping not to wake his little siblings. The door opened and the sagging face of his mother appeared. She always looked tired, her hair and clothes unkempt, with dark purple rings under her eyes. I guess that was the consequence of having eight children. I was lucky in a way because my mom died giving birth to me, so I don't have any siblings. If you can call that a good thing.

May showed up behind his mother, and could see in my eyes that there was something wrong. She just motioned for us to go outside, so we went to the forest and sat in a small clearing, ringed with berry bushes. I sat down on a stump and chewed my lip, wondering how to tell him.

"Okay, what's wrong?" he said, with genuine concern in his voice.

"I… I just… I was out and I saw this thing. I had an awful headache and it was like I was dreaming. I saw this boy… and he… he..," At that moment I realized that I might be going insane. What if there was something wrong with me? What if I was making that happen?

May wrapped his arms around me and pulled me into an embrace. He smelled like earth and something deeper, something I couldn't describe. His arms felt strong and warm, and I realized that I never wanted to be anywhere else. I just wanted to be in this moment.

Still in our embrace, May asked, "Was is a dream? Did you pass out?"

"I don't think so," I said, speaking into the warmth of his jacket, "It was almost like a vision. But how would that happen?"

"I don't know," he said slowly, thinking, "I really don't know. Can you tell me what you saw?"

"I saw a boy, not his face though, just his hair. Shiny hair. Silver. But not in an old way. It was nice.

Then this guy came and hit him, over and over again. I could see the welts, and hear him scream. But when I reached out to stop him, everything went black. Then I was in the forest again."

He thought for a while, and I just leaned into his strong frame. I listened to him breathe for a while, and tried to synchronize my breathing with his.

"I don't know what happened. But maybe it was just once? I'm not sure. But you can tell me if it happens again."

"Thanks," I said, suddenly not so scared anymore.

"Maybe you were just picking up radio signals from your ears." I laughed and shoved him away from me, and I saw a large grin spread across his face. I was just about to make a reply when we heard rustling in the leaves. Sar burst through, her face white as the paper so scarce here. She simply stood and gasped for a few seconds, looking as if she was going to throw up. May and I stood in shocked silence.

"Hestia, your father... is dead."

That was when the world fell out of focus. The trees were large blobs of color, and even though my heart was racing, it took everything in me to lift my feet forwards. Maybe if I didn't go back this would stop being true. I could wake up from this nightmare. Dad wouldn't be dead.

When we got back to our shack, I could hear officials talking inside. It was hard to mistake their all-black attire and guns as long as May's legs. They all looked like black blobs to me, their movements fuzzy

and unclear. I felt one of them guide me into the house, where Dad's corpse would be waiting. I faintly heard Sar saying that she would wait outside, and the he was in front of me. The tears finally fell and the world went back into focus. I could only see his face, pale and blank. This was the man that raised me, without Mother, without anyone except for Sar. I was alone now. Sure, Sar was still here, but I would never get to see my dad again. I would never read his books, watch him work at our old table. I would never get to hug him again, feel his warmth bleed into mine. I would never again hear him sing, let him wrap his voice around me and fill my consciousness. Suddenly the room seemed too small, to bare, and I became aware of the fact that silent tears ran down my face. I burst out of the hut, not caring about the officers behind me. Not caring about Sar. Or May, staring blankly. I ran into the forest, as far as I could until I reached the fence keeping us from entering District 20. I leaned against it, against the cold hard stone, and screamed. I screamed until I couldn't feel anything anymore, until there was no other sound. I blocked out the world with my scream, going until I just couldn't anymore. The I felt arms around me, and I didn't even care to look to see who it was. I didn't care about anything anymore.
I just wanted it to end.

Somehow, I ended up back in our house, with a blanket around my shaking shoulders. they took Dad away. They said that there was some kind of gun accident when he was coming home and was just in the wrong place at the wrong time. Sar and I sat next to each other, not saying anything, just staring at the plain wooden wall in front of us. We were both processing the information. Neither of us wanted to believe it was true. Apparently Sar was at the stream washing our clothes when an official told her. To them, it was an everyday thing. Almost everyone died during The Change, and to them death doesn't even matter anymore. I was just a thing that happened, totally natural. I wondered if they had had anyone close to them die. To have to suffer through this sort of agony.

The next day Sar told me that I was the registered adult in the family now. Since she and my dad weren't actually married, she was alone. I was the head of the family. Not very impressive to be head of something you're alone in. I guess before The Change this wouldn't be that big of a deal, but now the head of the family has to do a government approved job at least once a week. They say that it'll "build community". Sar does work in a corn field once a week, but Dad was the main one that kept our family going. I would need a good job to keep Sar and I at least relatively healthy. I told Sar that I would go to the work office on the border soon to see what I could do. She nodded, seeming vacant. I left the house and immediately went into the forest. I knew that I could find May there. Sure enough, I saw him on the other side of some trees, concentration spelled out on his face. I sat in a small pile of leaves, watching him do what he loved. He was staring at a deer, lazily chewing on some rouge grass. But he couldn't be fooled. It would run away at the slightest hint of noise. He reached around his back and silently pulled out a single nutty brown arrow. Its fletching was made from a robin's wing, and it shone a glossy blood red. He moved it so that it was firmly fitted onto his old bow, smooth from the oils of his hands. He pulled his hand back, and I saw the muscles in his long, lean fingers tense. In that second, he let go and I could see the arrow slashing through the quiet forest air until it found a home directly in the deer's eye. It was a quick and silent death. It didn't even feel any pain. In that moment I stood up, and I saw May turn in surprise.

"Ears?" he questioned.

"Yeah it's me," I said, running my hands through my dark hair. "I need your help."

"What with?" he was clearly interested now. I had gotten his attention.

"You know about my dad…" my voice trailed off for a second before picking up again. "Well I'm the family leader now and I need a good job to keep Sar and I alive and as close to healthy as possible. And you know about the jobs…"

"So you want me to help you dress up like a man?" he asked. It was common knowledge that he men's jobs paid better than the women's. It was a concept that dated back to the beginning of the human race. Apparently men are better and more productive workers, so they should get the better jobs. It has never made sense to me, considering the fact that I have outdone May in every fire-making, running, and berry-picking contest, and he's even a year older than me. But my thoughts aside, I needed to get a man's job.

"Yeah. I mean, I could choose a not so risky one…"

"Okay, but I want you to be careful, Hestia," he said, and I could see the sincerity in his eyes. He hardly ever called me by my real name, so I knew that this was important.

We walked back to May's house with him holding the shot deer above his head. He promised me at least a leg for dinner, which I thought was overly kind, but I would take what I could get.

When we arrived at his house, He handed me some clothes that he was pretty sure would fit. I told him that I would go tomorrow, and he nodded slowly.

I stood outside my house, testing the wind against May's sturdy deerhide jacket. I held strong, as I guessed it would. It was his hunting jacket, and he had given it to me for good luck. I had tucked all of my hair under a simple black hat, and my small breasts were easy to disguise under baggy clothing. I was just reaching the path that would take me past the river to the border when May walked up. He smiled at me, and I could almost feel its warmth. He walked up and said, "You ready?"

"I guess so," I replied, unsure of myself. "I'm just nervous."

"Don't be," he said, "The only thing you have to be nervous about is the fact that your ears are showing," he joked, reaching around my head and tugging both of my ears lightly. I smiled back at him, suddenly feeling sure of myself.

"Well, I don't want to be late," I pointed out, and May nodded.

As I walked along the path, I heard him shout, "Good luck!" and saw him waving both arms wildly. I laughed, waved back, and continued on the path.

The border was a whole different world. I could see the customs office inserted into the wall, and the job office that could decide your fate. I saw streams of people flowing about and around it, and the air was polluted with the sounds of stifled weeping and successful laughter. Guards were scattered around, directing people with solemn, still faces. I made my way up to the office, and didn't get so much as a glance from an officer. I was just another man looking for a job. Good.

When I entered the dismal stone building, I went in line with hundreds of other people. I watched the door as I waited, and saw light bouncing off of disappointed faces.

When it was finally my turn, I stepped up to a bored-looking man itching a patchy beard. With the most depressed voice it seemed he could possibly muster, he asked, "Name?"

"Hess Khalem," I replied, trying to drop my voice.

"Age?"
"Sixteen."
"Family?"

"Just me," I answered, and that got his attention for a second, before he continued.

"Gender?"

"Male."

"Special skills?"

"Observant and hardworking."

"Okay," he said, and I could tell it was a speech he had rehearsed. "We will send a letter to you as soon as we can. Expect it in five to ten days."

Official mail in District 19 was delivered by a hovercraft that dropped whatever letters you had near or on your house. And, considering that the only people we wanted to get in contact with were in our districts, that was the only kind of mail we got. In One and Two they were thinking of taking up an old custom from before The Change where you get your mail sent to a box on your house, but that just sounded weird to me. Not like an idea like that would ever come to District 19 anyways.

Six days of starvation and begging later, I got my letter for my job. I had been assigned border patrol. It was a fairly mainstream job, but that was good considering I wasn't really a man. I would start tomorrow morning. When I told Sar, she put on a smile that I knew hurt her and gave me a hug. May was very excited when I informed him. He hugged me and the lifted me off the ground and spun me in a circle around him. When he finally put me down, we were both laughing uncontrollably. I clung on to him for a few more seconds, letting my body remember how it felt to have his strong arms around me, then let go.

The first few weeks of my job were fairly uneventful. Not a lot of people tried to get to the border, and we easily stopped them when they did. My man costume held up well, and I was hardly worried about being found out. The other guards were more interested in politics. They endlessly talked about our new president, Hade Alou, and some shady gossip of how he killed his dad out of spite. Honestly, I couldn't care less, but I sat and listened because I didn't want to be a total outcast. I stood at the wall, a gun slung over my shoulder that was longer than my own legs. We hadn't been given much instruction about what to do when a person came along. We were just pretty much supposed to shoot. I wished that May were here, because he has been dying to try out a government issued weapon. I almost felt bad.

A few weeks later, I was on my job, and the day seemed as normal as any. Winter had set in, and I was decked out in a heavy fur jacket and wool boots. I stood at the wall, listening to the general chatter of the other guards. They were discussing President Alou, as usual. By now, their talk had just melded itself into a cloud of white noise, and the familiarity was almost comforting in a way.

Then, I heard a noise. It was soft, and it sounded like it was coming from right next to me. I heard a rustling of leaves, and a man appeared out of a tree about three feet away from me. I grabbed my gun to shoot him, but then I noticed that he looked like my dad. The man had the same black hair, amber eyes, and tall lengthy stride. I was taken aback. How could he be here? What was happening? It was if this man was specially chosen to be a distraction for me.

When the man got close enough, I could see that he wasn't Dad. The small details were off. But the trick had already worked on me. We were too close to each other to shoot. It was at that time that I wished I hadn't distanced myself from the others. Because now, I was alone with this odd man. He put a hand out to put on my shoulder and I twisted away as if his hand were made of fire. I wasn't letting him touch me. Thoughts raced through my head, and I felt dazed. Then, as if he were breaking some spell, he spoke.

"Hello, Hestia."

"How do you know my name?" I said, cringing when I realized that he could probably hear the fear in my voice.

"We have been watching you for a long time now, Ms. Khalem. We know more than you think." His voice was poison. It slowly leaked into my veins, taking all of the power out of me.

"Who? What are you doing?" I asked, my voice becoming more frantic as he moved closer to me.

"The higher-ups, Hestia. You wouldn't know us, but we know you. We have been watching many District 19 civilians for a position as a district representative. You will speak for your district, and control their -no, your- rights."

"I don't want to."

"Oh, come on, Hestia. Are you,"

"DON'T TOUCH ME," I screamed as his hand grasped my arm. It was tight and cold. This man was nothing like Dad.

"As you wish," he said, letting go of his rough grip on my arm with a jolt, "But I don't think you realize how serious this is," he said, putting down a small strip of white paper on the snow between us. I bent down to pick up the object, and when I righted myself again he was gone.

I stood there for a while in shock, staring out at the unchanging snow drifts ahead of me. After what felt like an eternity, I picked up the paper.

From the desk of Hade Alou

Dear Ms. Hestia Khalem,

You have been summoned for a meeting with the Officials of Ghensi for tomorrow evening at 0700 hours. A hovercraft will arrive at this time. This is not optional. If you are not seen by 0710 hours, a search party will be issued and you will be shot on sight.

I walked home in a daze, feeling as if someone had just punched me in the stomach. What would the leaders of Ghensi want to do with me? I was a lowly District 19 resident. No one cared about us. The prospect of having to meet with them terrified me, and I somehow managed to stumble home.

I stood outside my house, the cool winter wind blowing through my hair. It was the first time I had let it down in weeks, and I was somewhat amazed at how long it really was. I stared at the lightly falling snow, illuminated in the lights from the huts nearby. I could feel it twining into my eyelashes and slowly melting down my face. For some reason, the snow made me feel a sense of peace, even though my life might change forever tonight. I had no idea. But that was the difference in change. Some things are so great and powerful and overwhelming that you are scared, naturally, and think about how you could have done things differently to change it. But with things like this, there was no change that could shift the government's opinion. It was a thing that was immovable, and being scared would do me no good at all.

It was then that the huge metal beast landed before me, gaping its terrible silver jaws. The atmosphere was no longer peaceful, and I could see people hiding in their homes. But they had no cause to worry. They were only looking for me. A door opened at the bottom of the craft, which was long and rectangularly shaped, coming into a point so sharp you could cut your finger on it. A man emerged, one whom I guessed was my guard. I could tell that he was tense, ready to chase me if I tried to run. But I knew better than that. I stepped onto the craft without a word exchanged between us, and I could almost feel his contempt at having to guard a district 19 girl.

The ride felt short, but maybe that was just because I spent most of it admiring the interiour of the ship. It was like nothing I had ever seen before. In the back, there were leather benches on the sides, and the floor was smooth and glossy wood. The sides of the capsule were made of shimmering metal. If I tried hard enough, I could see myself in it, pointy ears and all. When we landed, my guard opened the same door that we had come in through. I was slightly disappointed that all I could see was a paved plane runway. I had hoped to catch a glimpse of District One while I was here. The man cocked his head to one side, and I walked in that direction, listening to him walk behind me. We enter a building that is so large that it hurts my head to think about it. Everywhere I look there are expensive glass fixtures, wooden arches and plush furniture. I can hardly imagine what it must cost to build something like this, much less furnish it in the way it is. But, then again, money is hardly a problem in District One.

We finally enter what seems to be a courtroom, but instead of desks and platforms to speak, there is one long table. My guard leads me to a bench, with a velvet cushion of course, to sit in which is right in front of the table. He then stands and waits at the door.

Just as I'm about to ask what's going on, a door on the front left side of the room opens and a stream of people in black capes emerge. They remind me of ravens in how their faces, clothed in shadow so that I could just see the outlines, are all long and pointed, their eyes sharp, noticing everything. Their eyes bore holes through me, and I wonder what I've done to deserve this.

They sat at the table, their hoods casting shadows on their elongated faces. The tallest one sitting in the middle , whom I assumed was their leader, said, "Hestia Khalem. You have been called here because we have a potential position that we would like to offer you. We would like you to feed us information about the residents of your district. In the past, we have not collected much data from District Nineteen because it has been insignificant to our governing. Now, however, your district has begun to pose a bigger threat to the health of other districts. We would like to know the inner workings of your district, and you seemed a likely candidate."

I was lost. I couldn't do this. How could I be a spy for my own district? "I won't do it," I said, my voice fluxuating with unplanned rage.

"I. Wasn't. **Done,**" he hissed at me, the words dragged out so long that I felt I could snatch them out of the air. "If you should choose not to accept our offer, we would have no choice but to take the life of May Sherringhetti instead."

"Why would that help you?" I asked, my voice having shifted from rage to terror.

"As you may or not know, Mr. Sherringhetti works in human development department in your district. He has been working for the past three years on a serum that will develop the brain to have a desire to do menial work and not lash out at us. Since all the information is technically in his brain, by killing him we can extract the information from his brain. This will work either way for us. It is your decision whether he keeps his life or not."

My dad just died a month ago. I don't think that I could take May dying too. I just couldn't. As awful as I felt to say it, I would do anything to keep May alive. I would consider the serum later, right now I just had to keep him alive. I sat as straight as I could in my seat, trained my eyes on the main ...thing and said, "I'll do it."

I walked over to my bed, feeling under the mattress, if you could call it that, for the submission forms. Sar had poured her sorrow into artwork, and now spent all of her free time in the forest, so it wasn't likely that she would find them. I sifted through the stacks of paper, flipping past the sheets already filled with notes. They had given me this invention from before The Change, a thing called the "pencil". I could use it to write down my thoughts, and, unlike a stick and berry juice, I could erase it, so that no one could see what I had written before. I kept it secret with my papers, my own special treasure. I was just getting to the paper that I wanted that my head started searing with pain. I let go of the paper, my hand going slack with pain. The world started to cloud up, and my vision blotted with brilliantly colored lights. I felt impossibly dizzy, and I fell to my knees, clutching my head. Just as I felt my limbs beginning to shake, the world broke in front of me and I saw the boy with the silver hair, now closer to fifteen, standing in front of a mirror, a large knife in hand. He seems to be alone, and I can't hear anyone else. He started whispering what sounded like a chant to himself: "No one needs you. No one likes you. No one needs you. No one likes you." He went on like that for what felt like an hour, tears forming into great orbs under his eyes, then streaming down his face in great ribbons. He finally grabbed the knife and raised it to his crest, hands shaking so hard that he could barely keep his grip. He planted the knife in his chest, first slowly, then fast, so that blood was streaming down his body. His screamed ricocheted off the tile walls, and the blood now formed a crimson pool at his feet. The last thing that I saw was him writhing on the ground, clutching his chest.

Then I was back in my house, lying on the ground, my head splitting open with pain. I started shaking, and was terrified. What happened to him? Who was he? I stayed there on the ground, thinking about my second encounter with death. It seemed terrifying that someone's parent would drive them to a point where they would want to kill himself.

Sar found me a few hours later, still curled up on the floor, still shaking. She picked me up silently, and held me in her arms. We rocked back and forth for what seemed like an eternity. Finally she asked, "What happened?"

I couldn't find the words to speak. "I... I had this vision and this boy... took a knife..." I started sobbing. Why me? Why should I be subject to this?

Sar wiped away my tears and asked, "Was it Dad?" Her voice wavered as she asked it. She had been a lot more like herself lately, but Dad's death had still left a gaping hole in both of our lives.

"No. It's not a boy that I've ever met. He was... different. He had silver hair and clear blue eyes."

"Hmm," Sar answered, and stood up to walk across to the other side if the hut. "What are these?"

I had finally stopped crying, but the sight of those papers made me start again. I couldn't say anything as she leafed through them, reading my messy handwriting.

"Hestia, what are these?" she asked, somewhat shakily.

"They made me. They called me to go to One, so I did and they threatened to kill May if I didn't do it, so I did and you aren't supposed to find those and what if they kill you too what if I didn't do well enough what if," I said, the words tumbling out of my mouth like an avalanche of truths. I just couldn't hold it in anymore. The secrets were killing me.

"After hours activity: Varri Leminis goes into woods at same time every night with a black bag. Salar Remshky leaves five minutes after, taking an opposite path," Sar read off of the page. This was just one of many observations I had been forced to make about my neighbors.

"There's way more detailed stuff than that. You don't want to know, Sar, I can't have you die too."

"I'm not going to die. If I do anything, I'm going to make sure that you don't die. Because I can't watch another person that I love die. it hurt you just as much as me when your dad died. And you know that. For far too long, I just hid from you, from everyone, scared to interact because I saw death everywhere. And then I realized that I'm an idiot. I am just such a dumbass Hestia. We are all gonna die. You and me and May and everyone. None of us can live forever. It is just a matter of when. So if I left you alone and then you died tomorrow, I would feel a lot worse than if I had loved you like I should. So don't you even try to distance yourself from me. Don't even try it. Because I will hunt you down, and I will not let you ignore me. God, I will slap you if that's what it takes. Don't make me do that, Hestia. Don't you even try."

I was laughing now; the laughter just seemed to tumble out of me as if it had been stopped up for too long. And maybe it had. The rest of that night was a blur to me, as if the laughter had put me under some sort of drug. All I remember is that I fell asleep with a dry pillow for the first time in months.

I woke the next morning to a soft thud on our roof and the sound of something overhead. I went outside to see what the noise was and was greeted with silence. I searched all around the shack, but didn't see anything. When I went on top of the roof, I saw a small red envelope with a heavy crimson wax seal. Mail delivered to our houses. Weird. Before I got a chance to open it, I was distracted by the sound of footsteps behind me. I turned around to see May walking up to where I was perched. He swung his massive leg up so that he could lift himself to join me on the roof. When he got there, we stared at the stars before he said, "I've missed you lately," he said, turning to look at me. "And I you," I replied, feeling a smile twinging at my lips.

"How is Sar?"

"Fine. She's been doing a lot better lately."

We sat there on the roof, lying on our sides towards each other. It was the first time that I had really looked into his queer eyes. My focus shifted between the worlds of green and blue, and I could feel electricity pulsing through the air between us. Then, the look in May's eyes shifted. I could read safety, warmth… love. He leaned in and obliterated the space between our lips. I felt the warmth of his lips cover mine, and the feeling was less a smashing feeling than a wave flowing over me, electricity being born from the pit of my stomach. I leaned in, and pressed my chest against his. My arms reached around his back and I slid one of my hands into his silken hair. I pressed my body into his, drawing warmth from his soft lips. When we finally pulled away, I felt so wobbly that I almost fell over. My knees knocked together, and when May saw when I was about to fall over, he grabbed me by the waist and put his lips upon mine again, and we stayed like that, his hand around my hips, my arms around him, our lips locked. Snow fell in our hair and in between our lips, but I didn't care. I was kissing May.

The next morning, I was woken again by the sound of Sar talking to someone outside. Her voice sounded taught, and she sounded scared. I quickly pulled on my boots and coat and rushed outside. When I got there, I saw that she was holding the envelope in one hand, and a crisp, faded yellow piece of paper in her other. When I approached I saw that she was talking to one or our neighbors, Varri. Just seeing her reminded me of all that I had done to betray these people. It was a fact that was almost too heavy to bear. Sar was saying, "But why would they send us money to go to a poorer district? It doesn't make any sense."

"Sense or not, I need that money," Varri said, with a note of desperation in her voice.

"Hey Hestia," Sar commented, turning in my direction.

"What's going on? What is that?" I asked, a note of worry finding its way into my voice.

"It's a letter that was sent from One. They are offering us money to move to Twenty."

"But why would they do that?" I asked, knowing of the government's sly tricks.

"That's just what I was saying!" Varri interjected.

"Look guys, I don't know. I don't know any more than you do. But we could use the money," Sar said, an answer within reason.

"I'll think about it," I answered, slowly walking off to my ever ongoing job as a border patrol.

As I was walking, I felt the familiar feeling of colors exploding in my head, the whole world trying to fit in my cranium. The world disappeared, and this time I saw the front hall of a mansion. I saw the boy, now in his teenage years, enter in the hall, with a bag slung over his shoulder. He was alive. I couldn't believe it. When I looked more closely, I saw hints of wrapping around his chest. The the man that I had assumed was his dad walked in, now dressed in a long crimson robe the color of his son's blood. He looked furious. "Where do you think you're going?" he asked, with a voice as hard as stone.

"Away from you," the boy answered, and coldness in his voice almost freezing the air around him.

"No. You will stay here. I can't have you leaving."

"I can't stand to be around you anymore Dad! You make my life hell. You know as well as me that I'm only alive by a sliver of luck. But were you glad? Did you rejoice? No! I just got more of the same old shit from you, and I am not going to put up with that anymore."

"You aren't going anywhere," said the dad, stepping closer to his son.

"Yes. I. Am," the boy said, his voice never cracking.

It was then that the dad took a step closer to the son and slapped him hard across the face. I could see the red hand-shaped blotch on the boy's face, and tears welling up in his eyes.

"You know what? I'm done. You can just sit by yourself because no one likes you. That's right, Dad. Why do you think everyone always does exactly what you say? BECAUSE YOU SCARE THEM," the boy's voice rose to a dangerously high level, "

AND YOU JUST CAN'T PUT UP WITH SOMEONE NOT DOING WHAT YOU WANT. WELL YOU KNOW WHAT? FUCK YOU. I AM NOT PUTTING UP WITH THIS ONE MORE DAY." He then turned around, and marched out of the door. The other man was incredulous. It was as if his son had never talked to him before. Judging by how he was treated, that wouldn't surprise me. The man ran to the door, ready to punch the first thing that he saw, but stopped when he saw his son marching off into the woods that most likely belonged to District One. He then vomited, his sour bile filling the front hall.

I was more flung into myself than awoken this time. It was as if someone had slammed my brain back into my head. Instead of feeling sad, as I usually do, I simply felt empty. I was beyond trying to do anything about the events that happened, but was still confused. I was becoming aware that what I was seeing was a story about some boy's wicked life. I was glad that he had broken away from his dad, but worried. I pondered these things as I walked to my mundane job.

An eventless week later, hype was beginning to grow about the letters. Apparently everyone in the district had received one. Most of the people were excited about the extra money. Varri had completely forgotten about her worry, and was now gleefully planning a feast for her family once they were settled in their new district. Some of the other families in the district were planning to move in together, and furnish their houses with a large oil stove to keep them warm in the long months of winter. It seemed as if I was the only one worried about this sudden generosity from the government. Even May was excited, and talked constantly about how amazing our lives would be in our new district. Maybe even a little bit too excited. But whenever I wanted to have him stop talking, I had an effective method of getting him to shut up. Kissing was a whole new world full of exploration and wonder. It seemed that every kiss we had got better, mouths open a bit, exploring the new lands that were each other's lips. I was in heaven.

About a week later, when I was with May, I felt my familiar headache. It didn't even scare me anymore. I was more scared about what I would see than what was happening to me. When my vision was clear again, I saw a clearing. It was fairly nice, with a fire in the middle, and a makeshift tent made out of fallen tree limbs and large leaves. When the boy, who looked as if he had aged a few years, was sitting on a log close to the fire. His hair had grown a bit, so it now formed a silver blanket around his shoulders. He was still as slim and pale as always, and I wondered for a second if he was finding enough to eat. But he seemed very happy. That could doubtlessly be because of the absence of his dad. He stroked the fire for a while, then, when it had died down to just embers, he got up and walked on a path leading through the woods. It was hardly perfect, but he seemed happy. When he was about a half mile out, he stopped to look at an aged piece of of paper nailed into a tree. It looked as if it had been there forever, watching over the forest. As the boy got closer to the paper, my vision got clearer and it got easier and easier to see what the page said.

NOTICE
BOY GONE MISSING
RETURN DEAD OR ALIVE
REWARD

And under the text, there was a picture of the boy, and a signature that was too messy to read. As soon as the boy was done reading, he took the page off of the tree, and ripped it to pieces with a fire that I didn't know I had ever seen. His face turned red with the effort of his actions, and when the paper finally lay in confetti around his feet, he slumped against the tree. I could see his eyes welling up. I wished that I could see into his mind. He put his head in his hands and the removed one of them to punch the ground with the same unyielding anger. He slowly faded out of focus until all I could see was a soft mass of colors.

The first thing that I saw was May. When I fully came to, I noticed that he was holding me in his arms. He was staring right into my eyes, and I could see the concern written all over his face. I smiled up at him, and, in an act of happiness, he softly laid his lips on mine, filling my world with the softness of his lips and the electricity buzzing in the back of my head.

I awoke on the infamous moving day. The day that my friends and neighbors would move to a foreign, poorer district for a reason that made no sense. Sar and I were two in a very small group that weren't moving. May was going to move over to Twenty in a few weeks. He was going to help his family get set up and then return to here.

I walked to work as I do on any other day, and stood in my position with my gun. Things were quiet as usual until I heard mumbling sounds. I quickly moved my gun around me, scared another stranger might appear from the melting snow, but it was just two guards to the left of me. I tuned out for a while, until I heard something about district 20.

"... It's brilliant, if you think about it. They're all so desperate and poor, they'll do anything for a bit more money. Get rid of the people, get rid of the district. One less to worry about. Its clear and foolproof."

"When is it supposed to drop?"

"Soon, I think. I'm gonna go check it out tonight."

"Ha. Imagine all of those poor suckers."

"Sucks to be them, I guess."

I was lost for words. It was supposed to drop? Something bad was obviously supposed to happen. And then it all clicked.

The money for no reason. District 20: the poorest. They were getting the people of District 19 to move to District 20. Blow up District 19, kill two birds with one stone. They were going to mass murder us. They could easily blame it on a military accident and no one would care. Everyone would just go on like nothing had happened.

I ran away from my post. I had to get home as fast as I could. I sprinted along the familiar path. When I finally arrived at my destination, I could see that my district was empty. It was a shell of itself. When I went to the path leading to Twenty, I could see one last shape leaving. I called out and Varri turned around. I had to scream for her to hear me.

"Don't go Varri! Don't do it! It's a trap!"

"Thanks for worrying honey, but I will be fine. You know me."

"No! It's a trap to kill you! Don't go, please!"

"See you on the other side, Hestia!" And with that she was gone. The very last person that was moving. I had run out of time. I curled up into a ball onto the ground, sobbing, until I heard the bomb hit. The earth rocked under me, and the sound of rapid fires almost drowned out the desperate screaming. I couldn't even bear to look up. All I knew was that they were dead. All of them. I would never see any of them again.

And it was all my fault.

"May! Oh thank god! You're still alive!" I screamed, collapsing into a puddle in his strong arms.

"So are you!" He said, sobbing into my shoulder.

He leaned back again and pulled me into a wet kiss, full of happiness and passion. When we finally let go of each other, I got to the more urgent matter at hand. "Is everyone dead?"

He nodded slowly, and I suddenly realized that meant his family too. His entire family had just perished in the span of a few seconds. His happiness at seeing me was fading, and I could tell that the thought had just occurred to him. The unthinkable.

I took him back to my hut and sat him down on the mat I call my bed. I warmed some water, and but in some herbs that Sar had found, making him a nice cup of tea. He took it and drank from it in long, slow sips, staring at the wall across from him with an unblinking gaze. We sat there for a while before he said, "I finally understand what you went through. With your dad, I mean."

"It is a curious thing, the death of a loved one. We all know that our time in this world is limited, and that eventually all of us will end up underneath some sheet, never to wake up. And yet it is always a surprise when it happens to someone we know. It is like walking up the stairs to your bedroom in the dark, and thinking there is one more stair than there is. Your foot falls down, through the air, and there is a sickly moment of dark surprise as you try and readjust the way you thought of things."

"That's beautiful. Did you just come up with that?"

"No, I found it in a book that was hidden in the woods. Somehow it stayed through The Change. By a guy that went by a food-like name, something old."

"Hmm. Well that's interesting I suppose."

"Oh come on May, you know just as well as I do that you love old things."

"I can't blame you there," he said, a smile beginning to form on his face. But I knew that this wasn't something that a few old things could fix.

"Do you want to stay here tonight? I'm sure that Sar wouldn't mind."

"That might be nice actually," he said, and put his head down.

I was awoken a few hours later to him crying out in his sleep. I looked over to Sar, who was sleeping like a rock, then creeped over to May and crawled under the blanket with him. I rested myself in his arms, and stroked his arm softly until he fell into a deep sleep. I stared at his still form, his chest gently rising up and down, then laid down next to him and let sleep wash over me.

I awoke to find myself in a dimly light white room. I tried to move my hands, feet, something, but they were all tethered to some sort of table. I cried out, and could hear the sound of my voice echoing off the walls, none of it leaving the room. Then, I heard a noise behind me and turned to see what it was. It was a door opening. When I turned to see what was happening, all I saw was a black silhouette, framed by the light around and behind it. It was tall, with thin, long limbs. It was just sstar when I had the signs of the headache. I tried to fight it, as the figure was coming closer. The last thing I saw was a hand reaching out to stifle my mouth.

I found myself to be in a room with the father, who was sitting in a large chair, looking over paperwork of some kind. I could hear a struggle downstairs, but it seemed that the man didn't care. He continued looking down until a woman in a tight suit opened the door and said, "President, there's…" But that was all that he could hear, because then a hand reached out and took her head and, in one swift motion, shoved her to the ground, where she lay unconscious. The father looked at her in awe for a second and then finally looked up to see who the attacker was.

It was his son.

The boy, whom should be referred to as man now, stood in the doorway, chest heaving with ponderous breaths. Both were struck speechless for a moment, until the man said, "Hello father," in a voice so laden with poison I was afraid the father would drop dead right there.

"Finally come back for my forgiveness?" the man asked, not a hint of fear in his voice, only surprise.

"Never," the man said, and reached across the desk to grab his father's neck in his long, slender hand.

"I see," said the father, now a bit scared.

"You wanted to kill me, eh? Find the prodigal son and bring him back to enjoy the fruits of his organs. Well you were wrong. For ten long years I have been out there, eating what I can find, killing innocent things to stay alive. Ten long years I have lived in solitude. At first I cried. Then I panicked. But you know what lies at the heart of solitude? Hate. Hate that has been burning inside me for my whole life. At first it was only a spark, but it has grown to a wildfire now, and you can't stop it."

"I see. But why take your hate out on me? There are plenty of innocent people out there to bully."

"Oh father, now you've just lost your touch. Why you? You know perfectly well why you, and I have the scars to prove it. I told you ten years ago why you, and if you weren't listening then, you had better listen now when I say that I will kill you, so you may as well say what's on your mind."

"Have you ever considered what it's like to be me? Your mom died when you were born. I had to raise you all by myself, and that was hard. I had the weight of Ghensi weighing on me, and then you just climbed right on top of that. Do you even realize how much stress that is? I just couldn't take it. It built up inside me, threatening to kill me. I just had to let it out, I just did."

"You know what my biggest regret is? That I didn't die all those years ago when I tried to kill myself. I should have just died."

"You think I don't love you? Is that what that is? Because I have always loved you. Always."

"DOES LOVE FEEL LIKE THIS?" The man screamed, finally losing his cool. He slapped his father across the face several times, then kicked him in the groin, all while still holding onto his neck. "Does" slap "Love" slap "Feel" slap "Like" slap "This" slap.

Groaning, the father croaked out, "No. No it doesn't."

The man pulled out a dagger from his pocket and put it up to the other man's heart. "Don't forget who you are, Hade Alou," said the father. Then the man stabbed him again and again, killing him in the first few blows but continuing to stab until they were both coated in blood. The man sobbed as he sunk his knife into his father's heart one last time, and the image faded from my eyes.

When my vision returned to me, I saw that I was now in a room I had been in before. It was the room where I had been questioned. Except that this time I was chained to a cold wooden chair. Not that it mattered. I felt that nothing could touch me after what I had just seen. When I looked up to the table, I saw that the raven-like figures were sitting at the long table. I also saw that May was with them, but he hardly looked at me.

"What do you want of me now? I did all that you asked," I said, frightened of their response.

"We would like to thank you in your generous contribution of knowledge that we used to bomb District 20. Your genocide was quite fantastic."

"I didn't even know what I was doing."

"Ah, but you knew it was wrong. And when it comes down to it, is there really a difference?"

"Why am I here?"

"We thought that you should know a few things before we execute you, for our pleasure. You are no longer of use to us anymore."

I sat in silence, wishing that I could leave, be anywhere but here. "What are you doing with May? He's innocent. Leave him alone!"

The raven in the center, who had been talking, laughed cooly. "Funny you should say that. I expected more out of a girl as bright as you. Do you not remember what I said that fateful day? I mentioned a job that May had doing brain research. It would do you good to listen."

"But what does that have to do with it?" I asked, terrified of the answer.

"He was ours. He has been working with us this whole time, you silly girl. I planted him to be a friend, but falling in love with him was a fantastic idea."

"What?" I looked to May for help, but his glance was icy.

"Griffin, why don't you tell her," the raven said, turning to May.

"I never loved you," he said in a voice much deeper than usual. The words dropped down on me like a heavy stone. "It was an act, Hestia. When you were young, you showed signs of great intelligence and leadership. President Alou put me into your life to keep an eye on you, to study your brain."

"You never even felt the smallest twinge of love?" I asked, my voice brought down to a whisper.

"No. It was all an experiment to me."

I began weeping harder than I ever had. May, or Griffin, or whoever he was was just acting. Those kisses were all fake. Everything I felt for him was fake. I didn't even know who he was anymore. My life was May, and now that had been ripped away from me. Suddenly, I felt anger lashing in my chest. Anger, and it was all pointed at President Alou.

"WHY. WHY WOULD YOU DO THIS TO ME," I screamed, not even scared anymore. Hatred had blinded my sense of reason.

The middle figure stood up and removed his hood slowly. Silver hair spilled out onto his shoulders, and his clear blue eyes bore holes in my head. His skin was cream-colored and smooth, and he seemed to glow from within. I knew his face. That hair, those eyes, so distinctive. I knew who he was.

He was the boy from my visions.

He was the boy who was abused. He was the boy who had to leave. Who killed his father. He was the one who killed so that his life could continue.

And his name was Hade Alou.

"It was you..," I whispered, hardly believing what I was saying, "Why did you do that to me?"

"Because we are one and the same, my dear Hestia," he replied in a voice as smooth as glass. "We are both creatures of sorrow, and lonesome, and betrayal. Our love has been lost in someone else, and we both have had impulses we would like to bury. Oh, don't look at me like the defiant hero. Some of us act on our impulses, and some of us don't. Your whole life has been an experiment, Ears, and every move has added another piece to the puzzle. I killed both of your parents.

"Oh, don't worry, it was quick. For me. I had to kill your dad so that you could concentrate on what was really important. I had to put in the May piece because you needed to know what betrayal is, my dear Ears. You see, no matter what I've done, you and I are the same. If you think on it. I am all of your awful impulses, too terrifying to face. And you are the part of me my father buried, kind and forgiving and clever. Emotions rule us, Hestia, emotions rule us."

And with that, he put a knife on the table.

Emotions rule us. I picked up the knife and knew what I wanted to do. What I had to do.

I picked it up and buried the knife into his unyielding chest. Blood spurted all over my hands and I relished in its warmth. I let my emotions run wild, sick of having to keep them in for other's sake. The beast that had lay inside of me had awakened, and was rampaging through my mind. I couldn't keep it in anymore.

Another one of the ravens, seeing what I had done, pulled out a knife and threw it at me. Those last few seconds of my life took years in my mind. I saw every detail of the scene before me, as if my eyes were heightened for just those few moments. I saw the blood of our president, pooling around my feet. *"He wasn't like me. He would never be like me."* I thought, in a last desperate attempt at proving myself wrong.

I wasn't like him-was I?

Acknowledgements

First and foremost, I would like to thank my writing group, Lucy Wendt, Signe Nettum, Ryann Chandler, Gwynn McKechnie, and Anna Feldman. We all wrote our novels together, and learned together that yes, it is as hard as it seems.

I would also like to thank Richard Hamel, who made this novel possible. He was the one that introduced me to this project, and made one of my most faraway dreams a reality. I will always owe him for that.

As long as I'm talking about people who made this possible, I can't skip over Lucy especially. She is the one that keeps me up on my feet, and I owe so much to her. If it weren't for Lucy, this book probably wouldn't be here. She is always there faithfully, even when I know I'm awful to be around. That's just how great she is.

And now for the classic thanks: my family. They were always very supportive, and helped me every step of the way. I also owe them for buying me the John Green novels that inspired me to go through with my novel.

Lastly, I would like to thank my characters, who basically wrote themselves. No, they were not fully based off of people in my life, even though I took traits that I saw in people to form my characters. I hope they seem as real to other people as they do to me.

About the Author

Eve Sidikman currently lives in Madison, Wisconsin with her parents, sister and her dog. Aside from writing, Eve enjoys playing the French Horn, the Guitar, and drawing. This is her first novel. She hopes to come out with more in the future.

Printed in Great Britain
by Amazon